Winnie the Pooh

Here Comes Winter!

A Random House PICTUREBACK® Shape Book

Random House 🏠 New York

By Kathleen W. Zoehfeld • Illustrated by Robbin Cuddy

Copyright © 2000, 2001 by Disney Enterprises, Inc. Based on the Pooh stories by A. A. Milne (Copyright The Pooh Properties Trust). All rights reserved under International and Pan-American Copyright Conventions. Published in the United States by Random House, Inc., New York, and simultaneously in Canada by Random House of Canada Limited, Toronto, in conjunction with Disney Enterprises, Inc. Originally published in a slightly different form by Disney Press in 2000 as Pooh Welcomes Winter. PICTUREBACK, RANDOM HOUSE, and the Random House colophon are registered trademarks of Random House, Inc. Library of Congress Control Number: 00-110038 ISBN: 0-7364-1180-1 www.randomhouse.com/kids/disney Printed in the United States of America August 2001 10 9 8 7 6 5 4 3 2 1

"Christopher Robin says Winter will be here soon," said Winnie the Pooh.

"Who's Winter?" asked Piglet. "Is he nice?"
"I don't know him myself," answered Pooh.
"But since we are having
a visitor, we should
give him a party."
"What a
grand idea,"
said Piglet.
"Let's go
tell the
others."

Outside, the cold wind was blowing the last leaf off the old oak tree. Several fluffy snowflakes floated through the air. By the time Pooh and Piglet got to Kanga's house, they were so chilly they had to stay for tea.

"Winter is coming soon,
and we're giving him a
party," said Pooh as he
sweetened his tea with honey.
"Oh, boy! A party!"
cried Tigger.
"Let's go!" shouted Roo.

Everyone bundled up in their coats, hats, and scarves and stepped outside. A pile of snow slid off the roof and plopped right on top of them.

The Hundred-Acre Wood was covered in a
blanket of white. Piglet, Pooh, Tigger, Kanga,
and Roo were covered, too.

"How will we get to the party?" asked Piglet.
"The snow is too deep!"

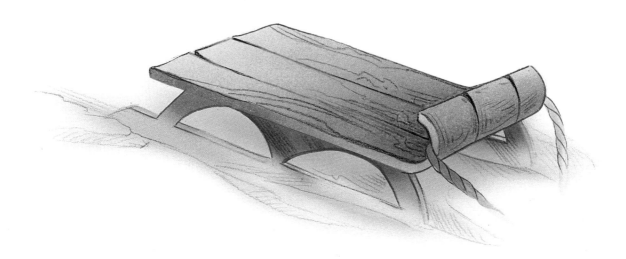

"Don't worry, little buddy!" said Tigger. "We'll go by sled!"

Tigger and Pooh pulled. Piglet and Roo rode. Kanga decided to stay inside where it was warm.

Roo reached over the side of the sled and grabbed snow to make snowballs.

"These will make good presents for Winter," said Roo.

Owl swooped by and landed on a nearby branch. "Winter has arrived!" he announced. "I heard Christopher Robin say so."

"Oh!" cried Pooh. "Do you know where Winter is?"

"I haven't seen him yet," said Owl.

"We'd better hurry and find him," said Pooh. Pooh told Owl about the party. "Would you fly ahead and tell Rabbit and Gopher?"

"And don't forget Eeyore," added Piglet.

"I'd be happy to oblige," said Owl as he took off into the air.

Tigger, Pooh, Piglet, and Roo all climbed onto the sled and slid down the hill toward Christopher Robin's house. They wanted to ask him where Winter was.

Tigger spotted someone
standing in the snow.
"It's Christopher Robin,"
cried Roo.

Pooh called out,
"Hello!"

But Christopher
Robin didn't answer.

"Oh, no!" cried
Piglet. "Maybe he's frozen
from the cold!"

"That's not Christopher Robin," said Tigger.
"That's Winter!"

"How do you know?" whispered Pooh.

"That big white face, that carroty nose. Who else
could he be?" answered Tigger.

"Well," said Pooh, "he looks shy. We should be
extra friendly." Pooh walked up to Winter.
"How do you do?"

Winter was very quiet.

Piglet nudged Pooh. "Tell him about the party."

"Oh, yes," said Pooh. "We are so happy to have you in the Hundred-Acre Wood that we're giving a party in your honor."

Winter did not say anything.

"Oh, d-dear," said Piglet. "He's frozen!"

"Quick!" said Tigger. "We'd better get him to the party and warm him up."
They all hoisted Winter onto the sled.

Tigger and Pooh pulled. Piglet and Roo pushed.
By the time they slid up to Pooh's house, the
others were already there. Owl had hung a sign
over Pooh's door—WELCOME WINTUR.

"Give him the comfy chair by the fire!" ordered Rabbit. "Gopher, get him some hot cocoa!"

Everyone fussed over Winter. Still he did not say a word. His carrot nose drooped. His stick hands fell to the ground.

"Oh, my!" cried Piglet.

"Maybe he's not the party type," said Eeyore.

"Our cocoa isss making him sssick," whistled Gopher.

"What are we going to do?" cried Rabbit.

Just then, Christopher Robin came to the door.
"Has anyone seen my snowman?" he asked.
"No," said Pooh glumly, "but maybe you can
help us. We brought Winter here for a special
party, but he doesn't seem to like it."

"Silly old bear," laughed Christopher Robin.
"Winter is not a who, it's a what."

"What?" asked Pooh.

"This is my snowman,"
said Christopher Robin.

"He's not Winter?" asked Pooh.

"No," said Christopher Robin.
"Winter is the season—you
know, the time of year. Cold
snow and mistletoe, warm fires
and good friends . . ."

Pooh scratched his nose thoughtfully. "Oh, I see now," he giggled.

Christopher Robin laughed, too. "Come on, we'd better get the snowman back outside before he melts. Luckily, snowmen are easy to fix." They undrooped the snowman's nose and stuck his stick hands back in.

"We can still have a party to celebrate winter," said Christopher Robin. "Let's have fun!"

Everyone threw Roo's snowballs. They took turns riding on Tigger's sled. They made snow angels. They caught snowflakes on their tongues. They sang songs and danced around the snowman until they couldn't dance anymore.

"Everyone inside for honey carrot cake and hot cocoa!" called Rabbit. They all gathered around the fire.

Christopher Robin gave Pooh a little hug. "Happy winter, Pooh," he said.

"Happy winter!" cried Pooh.